# FARM BOY

# FARM

# BOY

The Sequel to *War Horse*

by Michael Morpurgo
illustrated by Michael Foreman

SCHOLASTIC INC.

First published in Great Britain in 1997 by Pavilion Books, an imprint of Anova Books

ISBN 978-0-545-49683-4

12 11 10 9 8 7 6 5 4 3 2 1          12 13 14 15 16 17/0

Printed in the U.S.A.          40

First Scholastic paperback printing, December 2012

Book design by Kevin Callahan

For the people of Iddesleigh,
past, present & future.

M. M.

There's an old green Fordson tractor in the back of Grandpa's barn, always covered in cornsacks. When I was very little, I used to go in there, pull off the cornsacks, climb up, and drive it all over the farm. I'd be gone all morning sometimes, but they always knew where to find me. I'd be plowing or tilling or mowing, anything I wanted. It didn't matter to me that the engine didn't work, that one of the iron wheels was missing, that I couldn't even move the steering wheel.

Up there on my tractor, I was a farmer, like my grandpa, and I could go all over the farm, wherever I wanted. When I'd finished, I always had to put the corn-sacks back and cover it up. Grandpa said I had to, so that it didn't get dusty. That old tractor, he said, was very important, very special. I knew that already of course, but it wasn't until many years later that I discovered just how important, just how special it was.

I come from a family of farmers going back generations and generations, but I wouldn't have known much about it if Grandpa hadn't told me. My own mother and father never seemed that interested in family roots, or maybe they just preferred not to talk about them. My mother grew up on the farm. She was the youngest of four sisters, and none of them had stayed on the farm any longer than they'd had to. School took her away to college. College took her off to London, to teaching first, then to meeting my father, a townie through and through, and one who made no secret of his dislike for the countryside and everything to do with it.

"All right in pictures, I suppose," he'd say, "just as long as you don't have to smell it or walk in it." And he'd say that in front of Grandpa, too.

I have always felt they were a little ashamed of Grandpa and his old-fashioned ways, and I never really understood why—until recently, that is. When I found out, it wasn't Grandpa I was ashamed of.

I always loved going down to Devon, to Burrow, his

old thatched house at the bottom of a rutty lane. He was born there. He'd never lived anywhere else, nor had any desire to do so. He's the only person I've ever met who seems utterly contented with his own place on earth, with the life he's lived. That's not to say that he never grumbles. He does — about the weather, about his television reception — he loves detective series, whodunits, police dramas. He'll curse the foxes when they tip over his garbage bins, and shout abuse at the jets when they come screaming low over the chimney pots. But he never ever complains about his lot in life. Best of all, he never pretends to be someone he isn't, and what's more, he doesn't want me to be anyone I'm not. I like that in him, I always have.

That's maybe why I've spent so many of my school holidays with him down on the farm in Devon.

Sometimes he'll tell me how things were when he was young. He doesn't say things were better then, or worse. He just talks about how they were. I think it's because he loves to remember.

Grandpa loves his swallows. We'd often watch them together as they skimmed low over the fields and he'd shake his head in wonder. He once told me why it was that he loved swallows so much. That was when he first told me about his father, my great-grandfather, or "the Corporal," as everyone in the village called him. And that's when I first heard about Joey, too.

"Swallows," Grandpa began, settling back in his

chair. I knew I was in for a story. "Now, they must've been the very first bird I ever set eyes on. And that's funny, that is. My father, when he was a lad, used to go 'round the farms seeking out all the sparrows' nests and crows' nests and rooks' nests. He'd pinch the eggs, see, and he'd get money for that, for every egg in his hat. It wasn't a lot, but every penny helped. Sparrows and crows and rooks, they was a terrible nuisance to the farmers. They'd soon get at the corn if you let them. Anyway, Father got himself into some trouble, and it was all on account of the swallows. He had a friend—I can't remember names, never could—but a school friend anyhow, and this lad, he went and robbed a swallow's nest, silly monkey, instead of a sparrow's nest like he should have. Well, Father saw what he'd done, and he saw red. He gave him an awful licking, so the lad went home with a bleeding nose. Father went and put the swallow's eggs back. Next thing Father knows, the boy's mother comes 'round and boxes his ears for him, and he gets sent to bed without any tea.

KEEPS ANIMALS *fit!*

ELLIMAN'S ROYAL EMBROCATION

1/6     2/9     4/6

Not hardly fair when you think about it, is it? Anyway, putting the eggs back didn't do no good. Mother bird never came back.

"Father was always getting into scrapes when he was a lad. But the worst scrape he ever got himself into was the war, First World War. And just like with the swallow's eggs, he didn't want to fight anyone. It just happened. This time it was all on account of the horse. See, he didn't go off to the war because he wanted to fight for King and Country like lots of others did. It wasn't like that. He went because his horse went, because Joey went.

"Father was just a farm boy when the war broke out: fourteen, that's all. Like me, he didn't get a lot of schooling. He never reckoned much to schooling and that. He said you could learn most of what was worth knowing from keeping your eyes and ears peeled. Best way of learning, he always said, was doing. He was right enough there, I reckon. Anyway, that's by the by. He had this young colt, broke him to halter, broke him to ride, broke him to plow. Joey, he called him. He had four white socks on him, a white cross on his forehead, and he was bay. Turned out to be his best friend in all the world. They had an old mare, too. Zoey, she was called, and the two of them plowed like they'd been born to it, which they was, I suppose. Weren't a team of working horses in the parish to touch them. Joey was strong as an ox, and

gentle as a lamb. Zoey had the brains, kept the furrow straight as an arrow. But it was Joey Father loved best. If he ever got sick, Father would bed down with him in his stable and never leave his side. He loved that horse like a brother, more maybe.

"Anyway, one day, a few months after the war started, Father goes off to market to sell some fat sheep. In them days of course, you had to herd them down the road to market. No trucks, nothing like that. So he was gone most of the day. Meanwhile the army's come to the village looking for good sturdy horses, and they're paying good money, too. They needed all the horses they could get for the cavalry, for pulling the guns maybe, or the ammunition wagons, ambulances, too. Most things was horse-drawn in them days. Father comes back from market and sees Joey being taken away. It's too late to stop it. It was his own father that did it. He'd gone and sold Joey to the army for forty pounds. More like forty pieces of silver, I'd say.

"Father always said he was drunk and he didn't mean no harm by it, but I don't reckon that's any sort of excuse, do you? And do you know, I never

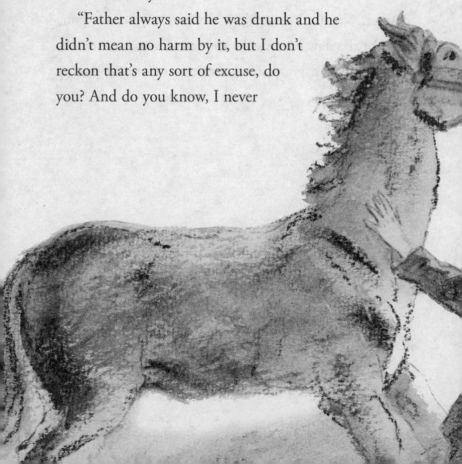

heard Father say a harsh word about it after. He was just like that. Kindest man that ever lived, my father. Big and gentle, just like Joey. But he had spirit all right. Couple of weeks later he'd upped and gone, gone to join up, gone to find Joey. He

13

had to tell the recruiting sergeant he was sixteen, but he wasn't of course. He was tall enough, though, and his voice was broke. So off he goes to France. Gone for a soldier at fourteen.

"Now, there's millions of men over there, millions of horses, too. Needle in a haystack you might think, and you'd be right. It took him three years of looking, but

he never gave up. Just staying alive was the difficult bit. Hell on earth, he called it. Always waiting, waiting to go up to the front line, waiting in the trenches with the whizbangs and shells bursting all around you, waiting for the whistle to send you out over the top and across no-man's-land, waiting for the bullet that had your name on it.

"He was wounded a couple of times in the leg, lucky wounds, he said. You were always a lot safer in the hospital than in the trenches. But his ears started ring-ing with all the thunder of the shells, and he had that trouble all his life afterward. He saw things out there in France, terrible things that don't bear thinking about: his friends blowed up, horses drowned dead in the mud before his very eyes. And all the while he never forgot Joey, never forgot what he'd come for.

"Then, at first light one morning, he's on 'stand-to' in the trenches waiting for the Germans to attack, and

he looks through the mist and there's this horse wander-
ing around, lost in no-man's-land. 'Course, Father never
thinks twice. He loves horses, all horses, so he's got to
fetch him in, hasn't he? Quick as a twick, he's up over
the top and running.

19

"Trouble is, there's a German chap doing just the very same thing. So the two of them meet, right out there in the middle, both armies looking on. They tossed a coin for it, honest they did. They tossed for the horse, and Father won. And . . . you guessed it, when they got that horse back and cleaned him down, he had the four white socks, he had the white cross on his forehead, and he was bay. He was Joey. Takes some believing, I know. But it's true enough, I'm telling you.

"And that weren't the end of it, not by a long shot. When the war was over, the army decided to sell off all the old warhorses for meat. That's right, they were going to kill Joey. After all he'd been through, all he'd done, they were going to have him slaughtered for meat.

So Father did the only thing he could. He bought Joey
back off the army with his own money, all the pay he'd
saved up, and brought him home safe and sound at the
end of the war.

"They had banners and bunting and flags up all over the village. Hatherleigh Silver Band, too, just for him. I seen the photograph. Everyone was there, whole parish, shouting and cheering: 'Welcome home, Corporal!

Welcome home, Joey!' Always called him Corporal. Everyone did.

"But once the celebrations were over, Father went straight back to work just like before the war—plowing, reaping, milking, shepherding—and of course he had his Joey with him. Everyone said he was so fond of that horse he'd never marry. Not room enough in his heart, they said. They were wrong, weren't they? Else I wouldn't hardly be here, would I?

"He'd had his eye on Maisie Coppledick ever since school. More important, she'd had her eye on him, so  it was all right. Married on May Day 1919 in Iddesleigh church. It rained cats and dogs, so Father said, and they moved down here to Burrow next day.

"One year later, give or take a week or two, and I come along. There was a swallow's nest under the offices—the eaves—right above the window of my bedroom, where Mother would sit with me that first summer of my life. Always loved swallows I have, since the day I was born. Always will, too."

Grandpa loves to tell his stories, and when he does, I love to listen. But it isn't just the stories I like—to be honest, I've heard most of them several times before—it's the way he tells them. He talks with his eyebrows, with his hands. And he's good at listening, and that makes me want to talk. He listens with his eyebrows, too. We just get on. We always have. I don't know why, really. After all, we were born into two completely different worlds. He's an old country mouse through and through, and I'm a young town mouse—bus at the end of the road, supermarket 'round the corner, rec center, that sort of thing. I don't much like *The Bill* or *Columbo* or Agatha Christie films, but when I'm staying with Grandpa I watch them because I like watching him watching them, his eyebrows twitchy with excitement, his hands gripping the arms of the chair.

But then there are times when he can be a right old goat. On days like that I just keep out of his way, and he keeps out of mine. He'd get to be suddenly sad and silent and never looking at me, and I'd know then. When he didn't polish his boots last thing at night—that was a bad sign. He wouldn't ever have the television on when he was like that. He'd just sit and stare into the fire. He could barely drag himself out of his chair to shut up the chickens at night. He was angry or sad about something, but I didn't know what, and I knew better than to ask. And then last summer, when I'd just finished school for the last time, exams all over and done with, and I was down on the farm for a while, he told me what it was.

Until then, Grandpa had hardly ever said a word about my grandmother. He had a photo of her on the dresser in the kitchen, and I knew that she'd died before I was born, that he'd been alone for some years. I knew nothing more about her, and I didn't like to ask. He was in one of his deep grumps, sitting by the stove in his holey socks, when I came in for my tea. I'd been cleaning down the cow yard. I didn't expect him to speak.

"I was thinking about her on the dresser," he said. It took me a moment or two to work out who he meant. "Be twenty years today. She went and left me twenty years ago today. Everything to me, she was, and she goes and dies on me. And you know what? We was in the middle of something, something we hadn't finished. And she took ill and died. She shouldn't have. She shouldn't have."

"What were you in the middle of?" I asked.

He looked at me and tried to smile. "You're a good lad. Come to think of it, you're something like her, y'know. You let a fellow be when he wants it. There's others that have guessed it, your Mum and Dad for sure, but her on the dresser, she's the only one I ever told. I told her before I married her, and she said it didn't matter, that there was more important things about people than that. Nothing to be ashamed of, she said. Bless her heart. She was shamed right enough, she must've been. 'Course, once I had her with me, I didn't need to do anything about it, did I? I mean, she did it all for me. And I had all the excuses I needed, didn't I? There was the farm. I was out working morning, noon, and night, and there was the children growing up and mouths to feed and rent to pay. Oh yes, I had all the excuses, but the truth of it was that I just didn't bother.

"Then, with the children growed and flown the nest, more or less, she said we both had the time to do it. She said we should sit down together in the evenings when I come in off the farm, and do it. And so we did. No more'n a month later, I wake up one morning and she's still in bed beside me. She was always up before me, always. And she were cold, so cold. I can mind I knowed at once she was dead. Weak heart, the doctor told me. She'd had the rheumatic fever when she was little. I didn't know it. She never told me."

He waved me into the chair opposite him, and looked me long and hard in the eye before he began again. "I still talk to her, y'know. Last night I asked her, I said: 'Shall I tell him? Would he do it? What d'you think?' And she was listening. I know that. She never says anything, but it's like I can hear her listening, hear her thinking sometimes. Like last night. She was thinking: 'It's about time you finished what we started. No use just sitting there for the rest of your life feeling all sorry for yourself. Ask him, you old misery. Worst he can say is say no.'"

He reached out suddenly and took me by the arm. "Well, will you?" I still hadn't a clue what he was asking me. "Will you stay here for a few months? You could give us a hand out on the farm. I'd pay you, mind, proper man's wages. And maybe . . ." He was looking down at his hands, picking at his knuckles. He didn't seem to want to go on. "And maybe, you could teach me, like she did. I'd learn quick."

"Teach you what, Grandpa?" I said.

"I can't read," he mumbled. "And I can't write, neither." There were tears in his eyes when he looked at me. "You got to teach me, lad. You got to."

"But you went to school," I said. "You told me."

"Till I was thirteen, and I wasn't bad, either. Few scoldings for this and that, but we all had scoldings, 'cepting Myrtle. Oh, she could read and write something terrific. Didn't help her much, though, did it? She went into service up at Ash House and died of diphtheria before I was twenty. Poor maid. Pretty as a picture she was, too.

"I never had the diphtheria, but I got the scarlet fever. I'd have been all right without the scarlet fever. Missed a year of school with that. And then when I got better, I wanted to be out on the farm all I could. I'd fetch in the cows before I went off to school. I'd feed Joey in his

stable, and old Zoey, too. It was near enough a two-mile
walk to school after that. I was late most mornings, so
I got a scolding of course, but I never took no notice of
that. Trouble was, I was always dropping off to sleep in
Mr. Burton's lessons, and he didn't like that, so then I
got a scolding again. And sometimes, if the brown trout
were rising down on the Ockment, I'd bunk off school
anyway.

"Harvest times, of course, I never bothered much with school. I'd be out in the fields, sunrise to sunset if need be. Hay in June, wheat in July, potatoes in October, cider apples, too. I'd go rat catching at threshing time, bash 'em on the head as they came a-skittering out. I'd trap the scoundrels, too, when I could. Father'd give me a penny a tail for that. And he'd give me sixpence for a nice rabbit.

"Father couldn't do it all on his own, see. He weren't ever well enough. Leg from the war played him up something rotten, and he still had the ringing in his head, and the pain with it. Mother helped when she could, but they couldn't have managed without me, 'specially at harvest time. Always something to be picked up, there was: beets, rutabagas—I do love a good rutabaga—turnips, too. And stones. I used to be out there with Mother days on end, picking up the stones off the cornfields. Weren't slave labor. Father paid me for every bushel I picked up, and I'd give half of everything to Mother for the house-keeping. But I was happy enough to do it. You ask me where I'd rather be, in Mr. Burton's writing lesson at school, or cleaning out the pigs? Pigs any day. Honest. I was doing something useful, wasn't I? Don't matter how smelly it was. Mr. Burton said I was a turnip-head, and if I wasn't careful I'd be nothing but a farm boy all my life, and I didn't see anything wrong in that. Still don't. And besides, I could read enough words, all the words I'd need. That's what I thought. I could write a bit, too. I wasn't stupid like Mr. Burton said. I just didn't like being in school, and I didn't like him much, either, not with all the scoldings he gave me.

"Trouble was that when I left school, I forgot even the little learning I had. No cause to practice much, see? Then, like I say, your grandmother comes along, and she can read and write well enough for the both of us. So I never bothered with it after that, until she told me I wasn't a turnip-head at all, and how she'd teach me. But we left it too late, didn't we?"

He sighed and sat back in his chair. "So? Will you do it? Will you teach me like she did? Will you? I want to learn so as I can write just like I can speak, so as I can read an Agatha Christie book from cover to cover. Well? Proper wages. I'll pay you proper wages."

"I don't know, Grandpa," I said. "I've never taught anyone anything. And besides, I was thinking of going to Australia for a while, after Christmas, when I've got some money saved up."

"Australia!" He chuckled and shook his head. "What a world it is!" He leaned forward. "All right," he went on. "Tell you what we'll do. You stay here till after Christmas, till the New Year, say. I'll do it in four months, easy. You'll see." I must have made a doubting face. "You don't think so, eh? All right." He looked back over his shoulder, a little nervously. "Her on the dresser there, she never liked me to bet. Chapel she was, said it was a sin." He was whispering now. "But I'm betting you one hundred pounds that if you teach me . . . let's say three hours a day till Christmas, I'll be able to read an Agatha Christie book all on my own, cover to cover, and what's more, I'll write you out a bit of a story of my own, too. You see if I won't. Hundred pounds says I can do it—the reading and the writing, both. So you'll have a hundred pounds more to take with you to Australia. Well, what do you say?"

We both got out the paper and pencil there and then, sat down at the kitchen table, and began. It turned out to be a lot more than three hours a day. Grandpa stopped only to cook, to eat, to walk up the lane at dusk to shut the chickens up— "fowls," he always calls them—and to sleep. The moment I came in from feeding up the cows or checking the sheep or mucking out the pigs, he'd be sitting there at the kitchen table with his pencil and his books, waiting. He'd barely give me time to wash my hands. To begin with, he learned all his reading from newspapers. He liked the large print, and the photographs helped him to guess a word sometimes when he couldn't quite make it out. Any new word he came across he'd write down in his book.

That way, I thought, he could practice his reading and writing at the same time. He found the writing harder. He said his fingers wouldn't do what he told them. Mostly he'd find ways to laugh off his failures, but from time to time, when things didn't go right, he would become very angry and morose, and then I'd leave him to get on by himself.

After a while I could see the newspapers weren't helping. He'd sit silent through a meal, dwelling on some dreadful story he'd just struggled so hard to read. One evening, after he'd read a piece about yet another savagery in Bosnia, I saw there were tears in his eyes. "Don't it ever stop?" he said. "I can mind Father telling me that there'd be no more wars, not after his one. It shames me.

It shames all of us. What's the good in reading, if that's all there is to read about?"

I tried *Farmers Weekly* on him for a while, but the print was small. And besides, he said, he'd done farming all his life, he didn't want to read about it, too. Then there was a rummage sale up in Iddesleigh Village Hall that produced sudden and unexpected treasures: copies of *Animal Farm* and *Travels with a Donkey*, and a dozen Tintin books, but best of all a dictionary and a magnifying glass. After that, his reading seemed to come on in leaps and bounds.

His writing was slower, though. He couldn't seem to manage cursive very well, so I didn't make him. He would print each letter very deliberately, pressing down too hard on the paper and often breaking his pen-cil in the process. He went through pencils as if he was eating them. But he never let up, not for a single day. Some nights he'd stay up till midnight and he was

still at it, and I'd be dead on my feet and longing for bed. When it came to the lessons, it was Grandpa that was the slave driver, not me.

On Christmas Eve at midnight he took me up the lane to the barn. "I want to show you something," he said in a whisper, and he opened the door slowly. "Same every year. Look at this." And he switched on the light. The cows on one side lay in their straw, blinking at us, and on the other side the sheep eyed us lazily. "All kneeling, see? Christmas Eve, and they're all kneeling, just like they was in the stable two thousand years ago."

"They're lying, Grandpa, not kneeling," I said. "And besides, they always lie down in the middle of the night."

"Do you want your Christmas present or not, you miserable beggar?" he chuckled, gripping me by the back of the neck. "Now, my lad, are they lying or kneeling?"

"Kneeling, Grandpa," I squealed, and he released my neck.

He smiled at me, sat down on a bale of straw, patted the straw beside him, and told me to sit. He took a book from his coat pocket. "I've got a surprise for you," he said. Then he began. "*Death on the Nile* by Agatha Christie. Chapter One." He read slowly, stumbling every now and again, his eyebrows meeting in a frown of frustration whenever he did. When he'd finished the chapter, he closed the book and looked at me, a smile of wild exhilaration in his eyes. His face was flushed with the effort of it. "You'll get two chapters a day till I'm done," he said. And so I did, sometimes three, and by the end, by New Year, he wasn't reading the words, he was reading the story.

A week or so later, I found myself on the train from

Eggesford Junction to Exeter, my rucksack on the floor between my knees. I was on my way home, then off to Australia sometime in February. I should have been looking forward to it, but I was not. I had been a farm boy for only a few months, and had loved every smelly, backbreaking moment of it. I had no real desire to travel anymore, nor to go to college, either. I had hated leaving Grandpa all alone down at Burrow. He had waved me off rather abruptly, a quick pat on the head. "Off you go. Miss your train else," he'd said. Then he'd turned away and gone inside. I'd just walked away.

My rucksack tumbled over at my feet. As I picked it up, I saw a white envelope sticking out of its side pocket. I pulled it out. There were ten ten-pound notes inside. The bet! The hundred-pound bet. I'd forgotten all about it. There was a note with it. It read:

I hope you like my story. I wrote it for you just to show you I could. It's about the old Fordson tractor at the back of the barn and it's about Joey and it's about me thanks a million for teaching me. God bless.

Grandpa

After a short search, I found the story. It was folded down the inside of my rucksack, just six crinkled sheets of paper, heavily indented with black pencil, every letter laboriously, meticulously formed, all of it quite legible. There wasn't much punctuation. We'd done capital letters and periods, but not much more.

# Grandpa's Story

When I was a littleun Mayday up in Iddesleigh village was always the best day of the year. There was the march around the village behind the Hatherleigh Silver Band all the menfolk following the Friendly Society banner blue ribbons on their jackets and Father standing a head higher than any of the others.

There were swing boats up around the village
green and a carousel and meat pies and toffee
apples and lemonade and then in the afternoon
we had games down on West Park Farm. We did all
sorts of egg and spoon races and sack races three

legged races skipping races. You name it we did
it. But best of all was chicken chasing. They let
some poor old fowl loose in the middle of the field
and old Farmer Northley waved his flag and off we
went after him, the fowl not old Farmer Northley.

And if you caught him well then he was yours
to keep. We had some fun and games I can tell
you. You could see more bloomers and petticoats
on Mayday up in Iddesleigh than was good for a
chap. Every year I went after that cockerel just like
everyone else but I never caught him.

I can mind it was the year that Father caught
him that it happened. I were maybe seven or eight
perhaps. He flew at Fathers face and Father had

him and hung on spite of all the flapping and
squawking.

We would have a good supper out of that and
we were pleased as punch I can tell you. Father
and me stayed up in the village and Mother went
off home with the fowl. There were a whole crowd
of folk in the Duke of York and as usual there was
some that had too much of the beer or cider. It
were rowdy in there and I was sat outside with

the horses waiting for Father. It was the drink that started the whole thing. Mother always said so after.

Harry Medlicott he had West Park in them days. Biggest farm in the parish it was. Harry Medlicott comes out of the Duke drunk as a lord. He was knowed for it. He was a puffed up sort of chap a bit full of himself. Had the first car in the parish the first tractor too. Anyway Father and me we were mounting up to leave. Father was on Joey and I was up on Zoey and this Harry Medlicott comes up and says.

Look here Corporal he says you got to get yourself up to date you have.

What do you mean says Father.

Those two old nags of yours. You should go and get yourself a proper newfangled modern tractor like me.

What for says Father.

What for. What for. I'll tell you what for
Corporal says he. My Fordson can plow a field five
times as fast as your two old bag of boneses. Thats
what for.

Bags of bones is it says Father. Now everyone
knows what Father thinks of his Joey how he won't
hear a word against him. Common knowledge it was
at the time. Well for a moment or two Father just
looks down at Harry Medlicott from on top of Joey.
Then he leans forward and talks into Joeys ear.

Do you hear that Joey says he. Joey whips his
tail and paws the ground like he wants to be off.
A bit of a crowd was gathering now most of them
as drunk as Harry Medlicott and laughing at us
just like he was. He dont much like what youre
saying Mr. Medlicott says Father. And whats more
neither do I.

Like it or not Corporal. Harry Medlicott is still
swigging down his cider. Like it or not the days
of horses is over. Look at them two. Fit for nothing
but the slaughterhouse if you ask me.

Tis true that Father had drunk a beer or two.
I am not saying he hadn't else I am certain sure
he would have just rode away. I dont think he was
ever angry in all his life but he was upset then as
I ever saw him. I could see that in his eyes. Any
rate he pats Joeys neck and tries to smile it off.
I reckon theyre good enough for a few years yet
Mr. Medlicott says he.

Good for nothing I say Corporal. And Harry
Medlicott is laughing like a drain all the while.

I say a man without a tractor these days cant call himself a proper farmer. Thats what I say.

Father straightens himself up in his saddle and everyones waiting to hear what he's got to say just like I was. All right Mr. Medlicott says he. We will see shall us. We will see if your tractor is all you say it is. Come plowing time in November. I will put my two horses against your tractor and we will just see who comes off best shall us.

Well of course by now Harry Medlicott was splitting himself laughing, and so were half the crowd. Whats that Corporal he says. They two old nags against my new Fordson. I got a two furrow plow reversible. You got an old single furrow. You wouldnt stand a dogs chance. I told you I can do five acres a day easy. More maybe. You haven't got a hope Corporal.

Havent I now says Father and theres a steely look in his eye. You sure of that are you.

Course I am says Harry Medlicott.

Right then. And Father says it out loud so everyone can hear. Heres what we'll do then. We'll plow as many furrows as we can from half past six in the morning to half past three in the afternoon. Hour off for lunch. We'll have Farmer Northley to do the judging at the end of the day. Furrows got to be good and straight like they should be. And another thing Mr. Medlicott since youre so sure youll win we'll have a little bet on it shall us. If I win I drive away the tractor. If you win theres a hundred bales of my best meadow hay for you. What do you say.

But my Fordsons worth a lot more than that says Harry Medlicott.

Course it is says Father. But then youre not going to lose are you so it don't matter do it. And

he holds out his hand. Harry Medlicott thinks for a
while but then he shakes Fathers hand and that was
that. We rode off home and Father hardly spoke a
single word the whole way. We was unsaddling by
the stables when he sighs deep and he says. Your
mother's going to be awful vexed at me. I shouldnt
have done it. I know I shouldnt. Dont know what
came over me.

He was right. Mother was as angry as I ever saw
her. She told him just what she thought of him and
how could we afford to go giving away a hundred
good bales and how he was bound to lose and
how no horse in the world could plow as fast as
a tractor. Everyone with any sense knew that she
says. Father kept his peace and never argued with

her. He just said he couldn't go back on it now. What was done was done and he would have to make the best of it. But I tell you something Maisie he says to her. That Harry Medlicott with his fancy car and his fancy waistcoat and his fancy tractor he's going to be worrying himself silly from now on till November you see if he wont.

But youll be the silly one when you lose won't you says Mother.

Maybe I will maybe I wont Father says back. And he gives her a little smile. Be something if I win though wont it.

In June we had a good harvest of hay off Higher Redlands and Mother didnt seem so worried anymore after that. But at home none of us ever said a word about the plowing match. Mother just didnt want to hear about it. I could tell that. But I can mind Father and me talking of nothing else all summer and autumn.

Father would say things like Well if any horses can do it then it's Joey and Zoey, and You come out on top after four years in the mud of Flanders like Joey has then you can win a little plowing match standing on your head in your sleep. I tried to believe him but I just couldn't. We went easy on Joey and old Zoey, worked them slow and fed them like kings so as their coats were shining in the sun as bright as a new penny.

And the plowing match between Father and Harry Medlicott was all the talk at school too. But I had a hard time of it. Everyone said Father was on a hiding to nothing. Even Billy Bishop and he were my best friend even Billy said Father mustve been mazed in the head if he thought he could win. And Id say something like You dont know Joey like I do or We got two horses and he's got one tractor. Or when I could think of nothing else I would just say Wait and see. But I never believed any of it even when I was saying it. I knew in my heart of hearts like everyone did that it were hopeless. Joey was maybe fifteen by now and Zoey twenty near enough but if theyd been half their age it wouldnt have helped. Horses cannot plow as fast as tractors. That was all there was to it. There was lots

of friends at school wanting us to win. Just about
everyone liked Father more than Harry Medlicott.
But even so they all said we hadn't got a chance.
And I knew they was right.

November the sixth it were going to be. I can
mind that well enough because the night before
was Bonfire Night and I was watching Father
sharpening up the plow for the last time and I
could see the fire from the big house up the hill
in the silver of the plowshare. Old Farmer Northley
had picked out Candlelight Field on Mr. Arnolds
farm as the best place. Three acres almost square

it is with hedges all around down by the river. There was people coming from miles around to watch and I knew we couldn't win not a chance in a million.

Itll be all right you know says Father and he smiles at me out of the bonfire in the plowshare. We're going to win. Youll see. He werent just putting a brave face on it. He really thought we would win.

Lets say good night to Joey and Zoey he says.

And wish em luck. And we did. I prayed that night like I never prayed before.

I was up at four o'clock the next morning to help Father feed up the horses with corn mash and hay. We brushed them down and went in for breakfast. When we had finished Mother had meat pies ready for our lunch. She saw us off at the door. She wouldnt come and watch she said. She had things to do about the house and she kissed Father on the cheek and went away indoors. Father

was a bit took back by that kiss and I was too. She
didn't do kissing that often. We walked the horses
down across Burrow Brimclose toward Candlelight
Field. Father and Joey together and me behind
with Zoey. It werent just the village folk that was
there it were dozens of other folk too from miles
around.

Like a fair it was down on Candlelight that
morning. Harry Medlicott was waiting for us hands
in his pockets and leaning up against his green

Fordson with his band of cronies all around him.
He had such a grin on his great fat face. I could've
kicked him. Honest I could.

Old Farmer Northley had us all lined up and
ready by half past six. It were gray all around but
you could see the field was parted in two with a
single furrow. As many good furrows as you can
plow by half past three this afternoon says old
Farmer Northley. The tractor to the Corporal if he
wins. A hundred bales of best hay to Mr. Medlicott

if he wins. And then he ups with his flag and waves it. Father calls out to Joey and Zoey and off they go up the field. Harry Medlicott takes his time gives the starting handle one good turn and the Fordson starts up easy as you like. He gives a great wave of his hat, climbs up and he's off too.

As the sun came up through the trees everyone could see plain enough that Father was already a long way behind. The tractor was plowing faster and he was turning faster on the headlands too. Father was falling farther and farther behind all

the time. There was nothing he could do about
it. But he kept going talking to the horses as he
plowed sweetening them on like he always did. Go
on then Joey. Giddyup. Theres a boy. Good old girl
Zoey. The crowd were on Fathers side most of them
anyways. Everyone loves a loser I thought and
there was tears coming in my eyes and I couldn't
stop them neither. They were all clapping and
whistling and cheering him every time he turned.
So was I. But it didn't do Father nor the horses
much good. I wanted to run off. I didnt ever want

to look but I had to. I was there at the end of the furrow each time Father came back and he would give us a smile and I would try to give as good a one back. That werent at all easy I can tell you.

By the time old Farmer Northley called a stop for lunch everyone could see the match was already as good as over. Harry Medlicott and his green Fordson had almost finished their half of the field. He had plowed forty eight furrows and Father had done fifteen. I watched Harry Medlicott as he sat up against the hedge eating his lunch with his friends all around him and I hated him moren ever. You could hear them laughing out loud clear across the field. I sat with Father eating our meat pies. We had a bigger crowd around us tis true but we hadn't got much to celebrate had us. More like a funeral it were. Joey and Zoey stood nearby munching into their feed sacks and then Father and me led them down to the river for a good long drink. They needed it. Drank and drank they did and we watched em.

A kingfisher went by quick as a twick he went and sat on a branch. Good luck that is says Father. He puts his hand on my shoulder. I am not done yet not by a long shot. You know the story of the hare and the tortoise do you.

No says I.

Well I do he says. And he gets down on his knees and drinks with the horses. After a bit he stood up and was wiping his mouth with his hand. Suddenly he's smiling. Theres a thing he says looking back up the field. She came after all. I hoped she would. Whats she up to.

And there was Mother walking around Harry Medlicotts tractor, having a good look. Then she was coming across the plow toward us.

Farmer Northley says you got ten minutes
till you start again she says. You all right. Hows
the leg.

Itll do Father says. Glad you came Maisie.
Horses are plowing well. They may be old but

theyre as good as ever. And then I saw Father was
limping as he walked away and Joey was nuzzling
his neck hair like he did.

At noon Farmer Northley waved his flag again.
On you go Joey Father calls out. Theres a good

girl Zoey. And they took the strain and off they
went up the field the plow cutting clean. I can
mind how I stood there and watched him my heart
full of pride for him and I breathed in the smell
of the earth. Nothing like the smell of new turned
earth. A cold metal smell it is, but clean and good
like the first breath of life.

Harry Medlicott was spitting on his hands and
rubbing them. Still laughing and joking with his

friends he was. He turned the starting handle over once twice three times.

Nothing happened. He tried again again again. All it did was cough and splutter. Father had done a whole furrow by now and was turning. Still the tractor wasnt starting. Then all Harry Medlicotts friends were running over to give a hand pulling this pushing that and they was arguing too. There was lots of shaking heads and shouting going on.

A little light of hope lit up inside me. I could hear Harry Medlicott shouting that they should get out of the way and stand back. He was hopping mad and I liked that. I liked that a lot. He spat on his hands and tried again. Didnt work. The Fordson wouldnt work. It wouldnt start. Someone else tried the handle then someone else. No one could start him up and Father had plowed another furrow.

A couple of hours later and the tractor engine

was in bits and Harry Medlicott was bending over,
his head inside the tractor his great fat bottom in
the air and I was as happy as a lark. Father was
plodding on behind the horses and I was counting
every furrow. He had done thirty five furrows by
now but I could see he was tiring with every one.
Mother and me stood side by side and cheered
him at every turn till our throats were raw with
it. I knew and she knew and everyone knew that

maybe just maybe a miracle might happen. Father
knew it too. He could see well enough for himself
what was going on and he was giving Mother and
me a bigger smile each time he came back toward
us to turn. The sweat was pouring off him and I
could see there was pain in his face now. Time and
again he staggered and stumbled to his knees. He
had to call the horses to a stop and every time he
fell he was slower getting to his feet again. He had
done forty eight furrows by now as many as the

tractor. All he had to do was keep going.

We had almost forgotten about the tractor.
We shouldnt have. I looked across the field. It
was together again. Harry Medlicott was waving
everyone back and spitting on his hands. He
tried the handle. The beggar started first time. He
clambered in and roared off up the field catching
Father with every second. When he passed him
a great groan went up from all over except for
his little band of cronies but I tell you that groan

werent nothing compared with the groan inside
me. I was sick to my stomach. Harry Medlicott
would win now. Nothing could stop him. We were
done for and we all knew it.

That was when Father went down on his knees
in the middle of the field and couldn't seem to get
up. Mother ran to him and I went with her. He was

looking up at her trying to catch his breath.

Legs wont take me no farther Maisie he says.
And then his eyes were looking straight at me. You
finish it for me says he. Let the horses do the work.
You just keep on straight. You seen me doing it a
thousand times havent you. You can do it.

Thats how I found myself following the plow

that afternoon behind Joey and Zoey. We werent
going to win but we werent going to give up
neither. You shouldve heard the noise that crowd
made. Filled my legs with strength of a growed

man it did. I never thought I would manage
the turns but like Father said the horses did it all.
I just did what I had seen him do and followed
the horses.

I was coming back toward the crowd when I
saw it happen. Harry Medlicott was turning fast
on the headlands as he always did but this time it
were too fast even for him. The tractor never hardly
slowed down like he should. He just keeled it over
in the ditch and leaned up against the hedge with
his plows plowing nothing but air and his great

muddy wheels spinning round and round. It were a handsome sight that. A sight for sore eyes. The engine choked and stopped and then there was a lot of smoke. When it cleared I could see Harry Medlicott jumping up and down. Like a mad thing he was. Well you can imagine the crowd was wild with it all by now and cheering me on. I plowed

on and on. Up and round and down and round
and up and round and down and round. I kept my
eye all I could on my line. I knew I had to keep my
furrows straight. I couldn't take my eye off them.
But from time to time I had to sneak a look at the
tractor to be sure he was still there in the ditch
where I wanted him to be and every time I looked
he was.

And all the time I was making up the lost
ground. I called out to Joey and Zoey just like
Father did. I was showing off a bit I reckon. They
two horses knew what was going on without me
saying a word. They were pulling faster and faster
never a foot wrong and together like one horse
with eight legs.

By the time old Farmer Northley at last waved

his flag for the end of the match I was so tired
I could hardly stand. When he counted up the
furrows Harry Medlicott had plowed sixty and
we had done sixty one. All of them good deep
straight furrows just like they should be. We
had won.

To be fair to Harry Medlicott he came right over

and shook Father by the hand and me too. Said I
was a good lad and ruffled my hair with his oily
hand.

Well then Corporal says Harry Medlicott to
Father. You won fair and square. It's your tractor if
you can pull it out of the ditch.

And by that evening with the help of a dozen

or more men we pulled the Fordson back onto
his wheels. We couldn't start him though so we
hitched him up to Joey and Zoey and between
them they pulled him all the way across Burrow

Brimclose and into the barn. They enjoyed that I
reckon. So the Fordson was ours forever and Joey
and Zoey never had to plow again.

Joey lived on long after dear old Zoey till he was near enough thirty. He had ten good years of retirement most of it up in the orchard. Loved his apples did Joey. Looked well on them too.

Father says to me once it's not the same working with a tractor. Cant hardly talk to a tractor can you. But all the same I can mind he looked after that old Fordson like a baby. Never get rid of it he says to me. Family history that old tractor.

In spite of his bad leg Father went on working till the day he died. Every evening when it was getting dark he would walk up the lane to shut up the fowls against the fox. Never let anyone else do it no matter how much his leg was paining him. And then one evening he goes off and doesnt come back. I found him lying outside the fowl house with his stick still in his hand. The doctor told Mother and me it was the best way to go. He would never have knowed a thing.

When my time comes I want it to be just like that. Good and quick. Maybe I'll be shutting up the fowls just like Father was and someone will find me outside the fowl house and the police

inspector will come along and look for footprints
and fingerprints and write in his report

Death by natural causes.

Fowl play not suspected.

Make me smile that would.

## THE END

Grandpa's story came with me in my rucksack, all the way to Australia. I read it by torchlight lying on my bunk in the sheep station. I read it in the bush by the light of the moon. I read it on the plane home, the paper glowing red with the last of the Australian sun.

By then I think I had already made up my mind.

I did go to college to study engineering as I'd planned, but four years later I was back at Burrow, farming with Grandpa. He's retired now, or as good as. He spends most of his days reading—Sherlock Holmes at the moment.

He leaves most of the farming to me. It's all I hoped it would be, and more.

I'd been spending my evenings up at the barn restoring the old green Fordson. It now has four wheels again, a reconditioned engine, and the bodywork is almost finished. My pride and joy. Grandpa came in to inspect it yesterday evening. He walked around it, patting it and stroking it, just as if it were a horse.

"Looks good as new," he said. "Wish you could do the same for me." And he went off to shut up his hens. No matter how cold and wet and windy it is, he still likes to do that himself.

Once he'd gone, I sat myself up on the seat. I gripped the steering wheel, closed my eyes, and off I went, thundering out over the farm. I was out on Candlelight and roaring along in the wind when he interrupted my dreams. He was waving his stick at me from the barn door, and laughing. "Mighty noisy, that old tractor," he said. "And you want to watch the brakes. You can't trust 'em. Remember what happened to old Harry Medlicott."

"I remember," I said.

For your Fordson

# AN INTERVIEW WITH MICHAEL MORPURGO

Q: *Where do you get your inspiration from?*
A: I get my inspiration from everything that is going on around me. I travel a lot and meet people, talk to them and see new places. I also listen out for stories and things that are happening in the world and listen to the radio and read newspapers. I try to keep my eyes and ears open, and my heart, too.

Q: *How did you begin writing books for young people? Did you always want to be a writer?*
A: Not at all. I wanted to be a rugby player — my dream was to play for England. When I left school I joined the army and then was a teacher. As a teacher, I had

to read the children a story every day, and my lot were bored by the book I was reading. I decided I had to do something and told them the kind of story I used to tell my kids — it was like a soap opera, and they focused on it. I could see there was magic in it for them and realized there was magic in it for me.

Q: *What was it like being the Children's Laureate, what did you have to do?*
A: I was lucky enough to be Children's Laureate from 2003 to 2005. It was an unforgettable experience. I traveled all over the country meeting people and talking to them and telling my stories. It was great to hear their stories, too. One of the most valuable roles of the job of Children's Laureate was the ability to be in a position to say something about the importance of books and the love of stories. To be in a position where I could talk about these things and people would listen.

Q: *How many books have you written?*
A: Over one hundred. *Private Peaceful* was the hundredth. Sounds like a lot but that's fat ones, thin ones. All sorts.

**Q**: *Where do you write?*

**A**: On my bed where I'm most comfortable. I pile the pillows up behind me, settle back, and write by hand with my exercise book on my knees.

**Q**: *Are the stories true?*

**A**: With each one there is an element of truth. I weave different truths into the same story to make another kind of truth. So with *Kensuke's Kingdom*, there was a Japanese soldier who decided to stay behind on an island after World War II, and people do hunt orangutans, kill the parents, and kidnap their young; and people do sail around the world on yachts, and sometimes they fall overboard. . . .

**Q**: *Are your characters usually based on people you know?*

**A**: They aren't usually people I know as such, but perhaps a combination of different people and ideas.

**Q**: *What was your first book?*

**A**: Shan't tell you, because it wasn't much good.

**Q**: *How do you know when one of your ideas is good enough for a book?*

**A**: I get a strange sensation when I know I have hit on a good idea. It's a kind of tingling feeling all over. I often spend months weaving my story in my head, dreaming it and living it over and over again before it is ready to write down, so knowing that you have found a good idea for a story is a wonderful feeling.

**Q**: *What is it like knowing that millions of people have read your stories?*

**A**: It is a thrill to me to know that people read and hopefully enjoy my stories. I love to see the magic that well-told stories can give people — there is magic in that for me, too.

**Q**: *What were your favorite books when you were a child?*

**A**: I wasn't the greatest reader when I was young and loved being read to, particularly by my mother. But the books I enjoyed reading most were adventure stories — *Treasure Island* was a favorite as was *The Jungle Book* and *The Elephant's Child* by Rudyard Kipling.

**Q**: *Who are your favorite authors?*

**A**: There are many of them. I loved the writing and storytelling of Robert Louis Stevenson, and Ted Hughes' poetry is in a class of its own.

**Q**: *Why do you often write about animals in your books?*

**A**: I think it may have something to do with the fact that animals are a good way into a story, especially for children. Animals don't judge like adults, they are accepting and will just listen. I have always been fascinated by the relationship of people and children with animals. I was a farmer for many years working on real working farms with the charity that my wife and I used to run — Farms For City Children. My respect and love of animals grew from that.

**Q**: *How long does it take to write a book?*

**A**: It depends on how well I'm writing, how well it's flowing. But I usually spend several months dreaming it up in my head — I call it my "dreamtime," the most important part of my story inventing when I try to weave the story together, do my research, and find the right voice for the story. Once I begin writing, I write very fast and will finish a book in two or three months. Then revising it might take another month. So, on average, a novel takes upwards of six months to write.

Q: *How do you choose your illustrators?*
A: By getting to know them. I've worked for many years now with Michael Foreman. Indeed, he's suggested many stories to me, including *Farm Boy; Billy the Kid;* and *Arthur, High King of Britain*. We really do spark off each other. I've worked very well, too, with Quentin Blake, Christian Birmingham, Tony Ross, Shoo Rayner, and many others. The publishers sometimes help in choosing who should illustrate what. They know many more illustrators than I do and can visualize a book better than me. But I know what I like.

Q: *How old are you? Have you got any children?*
*Do you have any pets?*
A: I'm very young. I'm 64 years young. I have a wife called Clare, three children, and six grandchildren. Sadly, our old dog Bercelet died last year so all we have are four

bantams, three hens, and a cockerel called George who loves to scratch up the flowers in the garden.

Q: *What tips would you give to young writers?*
A: The main thing is to keep your ears and eyes open all the time. To find out more about the world and have an inquisitive mind and heart.

# ABOUT THE AUTHOR

Michael Morpurgo is, in his own words, "oldish, married with three children, and a grandfather six times over." Born in 1943, he attended schools in London, Sussex, and Canterbury (at least one of which was horrible enough to inspire him to describe it obliquely in *The Butterfly Lion*). He went on to London University to study English and French, followed by a step into the teaching profession and a job in a primary school in Kent. It was there that he discovered what he wanted to do.

In 1976, Michael and his wife Clare started the charity Farms For City Children (FFCC), which provides young children from urban areas with a week in which they work actively and purposefully on farms in the heart of the countryside. They now have three farms—

Nethercott in Devon, Treginnis in Wales, and Wick in Gloucestershire. "As a teacher," Michael says, "I realized many children had little real contact with the world around them—to them the television was real. I wanted them to experience life at first hand." In the last thirty years, over 50,000 children from cities and towns throughout the United Kingdom have spent a week of their lives living and working on one of the three farms.

Living in Devon, listening to Mozart, and working with children have provided most of the stimuli Michael needs to discover and write his stories. He spends about half his life mucking out sheds with the children, feeding sheep, or milking cows; the other half he spends dreaming up and writing stories. "For me, the greater part of writing is daydreaming, dreaming the dream of my story until it hatches out—the writing down of it I always find hard. But I love finishing it, then holding the book in my hand and sharing my dream with my readers."

# ALSO FROM
# MICHAEL MORPURGO

A girl's search for her missing cat gives her an up-front look at the realities of war.

A boyhood spent on the front lines of combat inspires this story set during World War I.

A boy and his dog wash up on a deserted island—and discover that they're not alone.